Tales From Between Presents

Elin Olausson's Shadow Paths

TALES FROM BETWEEN

London

www.talesfrombetween.wordpress.com

Cover Image by Raggedstone. Cover Design by Matthew Stott.

More To Read

FURTHER EDITIONS OF TFBPRESENTS

Ai Jiang's Smol Tales From Between Worlds

Samantha Kolesnik's Lonesome Haunts

ALSO BY ELIN OLAUSSON

Growth

OTHER TFB RELEASES

Tales From Between: A Strange Literary Journal 1

Tales From Between: Words & Pictures

Contents

About

Tales From Between Presents is a journal dedicated to the work of a single author each edition. It features a handful of short stories, author notes, and an interview.

Join our Patreon and support this publication. It also acts as an eBook subscription to everything we publish : patreon.com/TalesFromBetween

TWITTER @from_between

INSTAGRAM @tales_from_between

CONTACT frombetween@gmail.com

Meet The Author

Elin Olausson is a fan of the weird and the unsettling. She is the author of the short story collection *Growth* and has had stories featured in *The Ghastling*, *Luna Station Quarterly*, *Nightscript*, and many other publications.

Elin's rural childhood made her love and fear the woods, and she firmly believes that a cat is your best companion in life. She lives in Sweden.

elinolausson.com | @elin_writes

The Editor Speaks

Hey there, *Strangers*, and welcome to this edition of **TFBPresents**. And what an edition it is! When we first started this project, Elin was absolutely top of my list to reach out to. She may not (yet) be a big name, but it's only a matter of time.

I first became aware of Elin Olausson when a small story dropped into my inbox. At the time I was looking for brief Tales to post to our website, and was struck by the writing of this submission from the first few lines.

On Excursion Day, the girls wear red rubber boots and heavy backpacks that claw at their shoulders. The boys trail behind, throwing sticks, laughing. Mr. Ander walks ahead, his neck flushed from the sun. They're heading for the Hill, which has a name that keeps slipping the children's minds. Simon Olsson claims that it's something to do with graves, but the girls know better than to believe what Simon Olsson says.

That was it, I was in. Sometimes a writer just hits you like that. You don't know the story yet, or the characters, but the voice, the writing, it just *sings*. It feels right in some way.

We're honoured to be sharing these stories with you, we hope (*sternly expect*) that you'll place Elin on your *must-read* lists going forward!

Speak soon, *Strangers*,
Matthew Stott, e.i.c, Tales From Between

The Old Man

Things happened to Marla's eyesight after she started visiting the old man in the woods. Not necessarily bad things, not to begin with. Just changes, and change was the reason she visited the old man in the first place. Everyone had their reasons, and this was hers—the cramps, the blood, the swelling in unwanted places. Life had been much simpler before and she wished for it to take a turn, or two, or however many were necessary to whirl back in time. The old man put his hand on her forehead and sang in that voice that wasn't a voice at all, and on the way home Marla thought that the woods looked different. She visited him seven times until she realized why. There was a juniper tree beside the path, and Marla used to stop and pick a berry whenever she passed it. The berries stung her tongue, sharp and bitter like the old man's eyes, and she ate them to ward off his smell and his ancient soul. They were a deep, bluish color, like the shadows haunting the old man's face.

This time, that color was gone. The berries hung lifeless, grey; she had to squint to make them out. She craned her neck, twisted her head. It didn't matter. The juniper berries had lost their shine, and she came home to find that the bruise on her mother's arm had faded, too. As if that certain shadow-blue was gone forever, and she could never have it back.

After that, she realized that she'd lost other colors as well. The deep sea-green of her favorite dress; the dreamish grey eyes of the newborn baby next door; the soft pink whispers on the underside of the begonia leaves. She asked her mother to see if her world had changed, too, but her frown told Marla all she needed to know. It was her, only her, and it was because of the old man in the woods.

She asked him about it a week later, after she'd lost the lilacs and the peonies and the edges of the rainbow. He put his hand on her forehead and sang, and the change ran through her. When she came home she bit into an apple, ash-grey and sour, and her mother said she looked as thin as a bean stalk.

"It's unnatural," she said. "It's unnatural, what you're doing."

But Marla didn't stop visiting the old man. She sank down at his feet, because there was no other place for her to sit, and she was tired. He put his hand on her head and drained her of color, fat, and blood.

"Tell me a story," she asked him. "Tell me about births and passings, about silver and gold."

The old man laughed. He sang in that language that was nothing like hers, and his grave-deep voice shimmered with precious metals. Marla came home to find her father's wedding bands in their usual spot on top of the dresser. They were lifeless, robbed of their shine, and the old man's laughter skipped through her head like a playing child.

Her brother followed her into the woods one night, as brothers do. Marla's shadow had narrowed just like her body, but her brother had no shadow at all and she didn't see him. Even while looking straight at him, she sometimes forgot about his existence—she had lost the sandiness of his hair, the cat-glow of his eyes. She went into the woods without thinking about Little Brother, and the old man sang, and the yellow of buttercups fell from her sight into his waiting hands.

Little Brother blocked her path on the way home. Marla saw him as a trick of the light, a ripple of fear and anger among the beeches.

"I want you to be like you were before. Not like this."

Marla laughed, because he was small and foolish and his colors were all wrong. "People change, Little Brother. It's the way of the world, and it always has been."

"Mama says you're turning into a bean stalk. One day we'll look for you everywhere, and you won't be around."

"She doesn't know any more than you do." Marla pushed him aside and walked on, past the juniper tree that was barely visible to her now, its greens gone just like the blue shade of the berries. She couldn't remember what those berries had tasted like, or why she had forced herself to eat them.

"Why do you go into the woods?" Little Brother called after her. "Why do your eyes look different?"

In her room that night, Marla watched her face in the mirror. It was gaunt and ghostly, and she loved it so much that she had no time to search her eyes for any changes.

The girls who had used to be her friends twirled through the village like fallen leaves, draped in colors she couldn't see. Marla sat on the floor beneath the window and listened to their laughter, and to the boys' names that dropped like birdseeds to the ground. She had been like them, a flare of light, until her body betrayed her and she was weighed down. She had collected boys' names like sapphires, and boys' smiles like ancient diamonds. Eli, Graham, Louis. They had all gathered by the river on slow summer nights, mouths tasting like beer and sundown, and Marla had lowered her face close to the water and watched her skin, her eyes, her grinning mouth. Eli had kissed her, then Graham, then Louis. The girls had sung and she had joined in, believing that she would stay the same forever. When the first changes rippled through her, she pretended not to notice. Everyone else became better, prettier, more defined, as if adulthood was all gloss and shine. Marla didn't become anything. Her new face was blotchy, covered in pimples that burst and left her scarred. None of her silky dresses fit her widening hips, and the boys leered at the lumps growing on her chest, their smiles nothing like precious gems. She cried the first time she bled, and when her mother explained for how long the bleeding would continue she cried more. There were no more nights by the river, because the old Marla was gone and someone new had taken over her body. She started dressing in black, in heavy fabrics that swallowed her and blurred her out.

"Why don't you ever invite your friends over anymore?" her mother had asked, as if she didn't know. As if she didn't notice that Marla had turned into something different, something that no one wanted to be friends with.

But it was from the other girls that she had found out about the old man in the woods. They had whispered to each other during class, their voices like tiny birds whirring over Marla's head.

"Did you hear that Lara Eve got pregnant?"

The air electrified with girl-giggles. Lara Eve was three years older, with a bearded boyfriend and skin that smelled like rose petals.

"But she went to the old man, and he got rid of it for her."

Marla had watched the teacher draw chalk lines on the blackboard, but she didn't hear anything except the hushed voices around her.

"Who is he? How long has he been out there?"

They had stopped giggling. Their silence reminded Marla that they were all little girls just like her, and there were things that scared them.

"No one knows. But he can sense what you need, and he'll give it to you. If you dare to seek him out."

"Is he dangerous?" a voice had said. Marla was shocked when she realized it was her own.

The girls had been silent around her, shifting uncomfortably in their seats. Their eyes burned her and she knew they were all thinking about how ugly she had become.

"Only if you've got something to lose," one of them had answered her question. In that moment, Marla knew what she had to do.

She kept visiting the old man every night, while her family were having supper at the oaken table, beeswax candles sweetening the air. Marla dropped to the ground at the old man's feet, and he sang about darkness and greed. His hands touched her hair and face, and she smiled because her cheeks were hollows for his fingertips to bury themselves in. On the way back she had to walk slowly, because her head felt light and her field of vision was swarming with blacks and greys and little else. She sensed shapes moving around her, hands landing on her arms and shoulders. But they were not the hands of the old man, and she shrugged them off.

She went into the woods for the last time the next evening. Her surroundings had turned to mud. Gone were the cramps, the blood, and the swelling in unwanted places. Gone were the berries, the apples, and the edges of the rainbow. She stumbled into the woods, thin as a bean stalk, and fell to the old man's feet. He grabbed her head and started singing, his voice piercing her skin. Marla turned her head up to look into his eyes, his ancient eyes that knew everything about her, and her world went black.

Previously published in The Ghastling Book Fifteen, 2022

AUTHOR NOTE

This story was originally written for a submission call where the theme was color. I saw before me a desperate girl allowing an evil being to drain her of life, little by little until there is nothing left. She loses the ability of seeing colors, but she thinks it's a fair price to pay if she can only go back to how she used to be—before puberty. The story is really about body dysmorphia and how it can ruin someone's life.

Questions From Between

BACKSTORY

How old were you when you first started to think of yourself as a writer? I can vividly remember writing a story about children hunting the Loch Ness Monster when I was 7 or 8 in school thinking 'I'm good at this, this is me'.

I was the same age when I told my teacher I wanted to become a writer, and I remember writing a lot early on. When I was 12 I started writing my first novel, and after that writing really became an important part of my life and something that I spent a lot of time doing.

What was your favourite book as a child?

I had so many favourites! One was *The Neverending Story* by Michael Ende, which remains one of the books I love the most.

Have you always been attracted to dark stories?

Absolutely. I always loved the darkest fairytales, the scariest cartoons, though they also made me really, really frightened and gave me nightmares. I read something recently about people being drawn to horror because they want to prepare themselves for bad situations, and that makes sense to me since I'm a terribly anxious person who's always expecting the worst. As long as it's dark, I'm interested, and I often feel cheated if a book or movie is not as dark as I thought it would be.

Who is your favourite non-horror author?

Swedish author Selma Lagerlöf, who was the first woman to receive the Nobel Prize in 1909. A master storyteller who has inspired me a lot.

You're from Sweden, what from your country or culture do you think has overtly influenced your writing?

I grew up rurally and I've recently moved back to the countryside, and I think that growing up in a small village, with the woods close by, has shaped me in a lot of ways. Many Swedes are fond of nature and spending time outdoors, and I've written many stories where nature and animals play an important part.

Do you recall the first Book/TV Show/Film that scared you?

I watched *Gremlins* at a young age and was absolutely terrified of it. The children's TV series *Are You Afraid of the Dark?* was another early encounter with horror that I loved, even though it gave me nightmares.

What do those close to you think of your writing career?

They are all very proud and supportive, although my mom wishes that I'd write more stories in Swedish.

Who are your favourite horror authors?

This is such a difficult question! I read all of Poppy Z. Brite's books in my teens and still love them a lot. As a psychological horror writer, I naturally adore Shirley Jackson. I'm also very fond of classics in general, and I'll never grow tired of Poe, Lovecraft and William Hope Hodgson. Some contemporary horror writers I love are Laura Purcell and John Ajvide Lindqvist.

Is there anything for you that would denote a particularly 'Swedish' style or type of horror?

Swedish publishers tend to shy away from speculative fiction, so horror isn't a big genre here even though it's getting better. But we have some terrific horror writers like John Ajvide Lindqvist and Mats Strandberg, and one thing that is significant for Swedish horror, and Swedish fiction in general, is social realism. Stories about ordinary people, people who are struggling to get by and whose lack of money means they have no way out of a bad situation. Themes like that work really well within the horror genre, I think.

Do you tell people in your day-to-day life that you're a writer? (I admit, I don't often reveal that I'm a writer or publisher...)

It depends on who I'm talking to. I'm a very private person and I don't like talking about my writing with people unless they are writers themselves or have a genuine interest in horror. My friends and family are all very supportive, though!

When did you first have a story published?

The first story I published was not just one story but a whole short story collection that my dad helped me publish in 2005. It was a tiny book containing eight stories, and it's not available anymore but might still be around in a couple of Swedish libraries. The first story I published in English was Scar, which was in Belladonna Publishing's anthology Black Apples in 2014. The publisher accepted stories in English, Swedish, and Norwegian, so I submitted a Swedish story and it was translated for the anthology. After that, I didn't start submitting stories to international markets again until the end of 2019, when I began submitting regularly.

What/who do you think influences your work?

My dad is a historian so I grew up hearing a lot of stories about local murders, paranormal encounters and the like. History has always interested me, and I've always felt a connection to the past. I'm also influenced by nature since I grew up in a rural area and recently moved back there.

Do you submit a lot, or are you more selective?

I am quite selective these days, and I won't submit unless I really want to work with the publisher in question.

If you had to choose three stories of your own that best encapsulate you as a writer, which would they be?

Such a difficult question! There are many stories I could pick, but I will choose these three:

The Moor (Featured in my collection Growth and in Luna Station Quarterly, Issue 045)

Razor, Knife (Featured in Growth and in Unburied: A Collection of Queer Dark Fiction)

Roadkill (Featured in Growth and in Nightscript 7)

What made you decide on these particular stories for this mini-collection?

I aimed for a good mix of stories—some long, some short, some new, and some previously published. Scar, being a fantasy story, is a bit different from what I usually write, but I really wanted to include it since it was published nine years ago and I wanted more people to be able to read it.

love

Before my mother met Mats and everything went to hell, we used to live in town. The neighbors rowed at night and strange boys sold drugs on the basement stairs, but my room had bottle-green walls and a window sill wide enough to curl up on. I still keep that apartment inside me, like a dollhouse snugly wrapped in my brain. If I could crack open my skull and step inside, I imagine I'd be a lot happier.

I hadn't been back for her funeral. People talked, I bet, but I wasn't in a very good place then and I didn't have the fare. One of her co-workers had sent me a blurry cell phone snapshot of her grave, names and numbers scarring the granite. No sentimental quote, no hearts or doves. *Angel-birds*, my mother used to call them. *Soul-carriers*. I stored all of her words in my dollhouse brain, on shelves labelled *good* or *weird* or *scary*. Sometimes the words got jumbled up, until I wasn't sure if they had hatched in her mind or mine.

The bus ride from town took thirty minutes. The road stretched out like a snake, fat and lazy after a meal. I listened to the same songs I had always listened to, my wailing girls, my mad-eyed women. Apart from the driver, I was the only one there. The woods glowered as if it knew I didn't belong. My mother was dead and I had nothing tethering me to this place, nothing but a dreamland apartment and a patch of graveyard dirt. I didn't want to come back, but there were circumstances. There are always circumstances.

When I pushed the yellow *STOP* button, the driver caught my eye in the rearview mirror. He was young, looked like a child dressed up in cap and uniform.

"What are you going to do out here?"

A normal person would have smiled, I guess, made a joking retort about hiking, but I grabbed my backpack and got off. As I watched the bus leave, it dawned on me that Mats might be away. He might refuse to see me. It wasn't he who had told me the news about my mother, but some distant relation I remembered only vaguely from childhood parties. Her breath had smelled like menthol cigarettes, but when I tried to picture her face it was just a blur of teeth and turquoise eyeshadow. Mats hadn't called me once. He'd sent me an e-mail about stuff that had been my mother's, shoes and purses he thought I might want. The e-mail was badly written, misspelled and blunt. It made me embarrassed for him and I never replied.

The wind braided itself into my hair as I went up the dirt road. I recognized it from my mother's description: never-ending, narrow, and cold. I don't know how a road can be cold but this one was, shivery like November. I untangled my curls as I walked, and the wind immediately messed them up again. My mother had used to tell me that I had troll hair, coarse and thick like bristle. She read me stories about changelings and I thought they were about me, about my burliness and the way my voice was never quite there when I needed it. But when I told her that she laughed and said my thoughts were too large for my head.

The house was isolated, dropped in the middle of the woods as if by mistake. I had never seen it before, not even in a photo. My mother had lived here for five years and I hadn't been to see her once. She used to tell me little things whenever we talked on the phone. *Today there was a squirrel on the bird-feeder. I tapped the window but it just kept eating*. I never wanted to imagine her new life, the house she had chosen in favor of our apartment. The man. Seeing the house now, I couldn't understand why she had wanted to live here. It had dust-grey asbestos siding and red brick pillars on the porch, which had room for little more than a plastic chair. The yard was crammed with rusty cars with doors or tires missing, lined up like broken toys. The barn and sheds needed paint. Deer skulls and antlers hung over the barn doors, like flashes of white light against the greying wood. I walked on, thinking about that one time when Mats and I had met. We had been in a restaurant in town, celebrating my mother's birthday. She had worn her velvet dress, Mats had made eyes at the waitress, and I had refused to utter a word. The day after, she got a tattoo on her wrist that read *love*. It got infected, never healed properly, and she started wearing long sleeves to cover it up.

A noise wormed toward me as I went through the gate, a pathetic whine that made me think of puppies. The old lady who had lived across from us had had a puppy, but it got sick and died. Its fur had been golden brown, like melting sugar.

Mats pushed the door open as I stepped onto the porch. I saw the square window in the door and realized that he had been spying through it, calmly waiting for me to come closer. He looked as I had remembered, not that I did remember much. I had crossed him out with black marker but here he was, whiskers, leather vest. There was a smell, a blend of cooking and motor oil and cheap beer. My mother had always loathed the smell of beer.

"Caroline? This is a surprise." He scratched his big belly. It made my skin itch and I wished I hadn't come.

"Hi." The house seemed to steal the word, snatch it from me and gobble it up. It was old, had been in Mats' family for generations. During that awful dinner, he had bragged about his great-grandfather who had built the house, the barn and sheds. *The place is ours and always will be.*

"Care to tell me why you're here?" His eyes were small and red-rimmed. They gave me bad thoughts.

"You wrote that e-mail. About her things."

Mats huffed. "That was what, two years ago? You must've been busy."

"School," I said. My tongue moved behind my lips, dry and swollen like a cloth. "I'm here now."

"For how long?"

My dorm room flashed through my brain. The silverfish, the cedar incense, the mess on the bathroom floor. "Only a few weeks. At most." The thought of living in his home made me sick. *He's a good man*, my mother had said. *You'll find out once you get to know him.*

"Isn't that something." Mats watched me for a long while. His hand on the doorframe was meaty, the skin red. "And what exactly do I get out of it?"

"I'm a great cook," I lied. I was nothing like my mother, who had spent her weekends making sourdough bread and creamy chicken stews. I vividly remembered the open-wound red of the canned tomatoes she used to buy whenever they were on sale. Tomatoes, peas, mushy baby carrots. All the little things my mother kept in jars and bottles.

"Okay." He narrowed his eyes, and I had the feeling that he was peeling my skin away. Calmly, with tweezers. "Stay a while, then. Suppose I can't deny you, since you're Yvonne's kid."

I didn't like the way he used my mother's name. Come to think of it, I had never liked it when people used her name. It made her seem like a different person, someone who wasn't attached to me.

"Just one thing, Caroline." Mats watched as I unlaced my boots. His stench stuck to my skin like an oily film, and my fingers slipped. "Curfew starts at ten PM. I don't want you running around at night."

"I'm twenty-six," I told him. "I'm an adult."

"My house, my rules." His smile didn't match the tombstone granite in his voice. Without arguing any further I went into the sad kitchen, which was all seventies wallpaper and yellowed linoleum. Mats came after me, humming cheerfully.

"It's not much, as you can see. And you'll only get a cell reception here and in the living room, I'm sorry to say. The woods don't like modern-day technology." He grinned, showing a missing tooth. It made his face skewed, and I couldn't look away from it.

"I don't use my phone a lot anyway."

"You're a strange young woman, then," Mats said. "You can take the guestroom while you're here. Yvonne decorated it for you, but you never came."

The guestroom at the end of the hall was painted pink, with framed horse posters on the walls. The bed creaked when I sat down on it, a helpless little sound that made me irrationally angry. I didn't want to be here but now I was, in this weepy pre-teen room that was nothing like my dollhouse. My mother should have known that I couldn't stand pink.

"Hungry?" Mats stood in the doorway, studying my face. The smile was back, the missing-tooth grin. "There's some meat sauce left."

In my head, I curled up on the window sill in my bottle-green room and waited for my mother to come home. Read me stories and promise to never leave.

Mats had a friend over that night. An old man who didn't introduce himself, with a thick accent and muddy boots that stained the kitchen floor. They sat in there, drank, watched video clips on Mats' phone. At a quarter past ten I went to the kitchen to get a glass of water, and Mats shot me a look.

"Curfew," he said. I drank the water and went back to my room. Slipped into that narrow bed and had bad dreams about horses. When I woke up the next morning, the old man was gone. Mats was out in the yard chopping wood. I watched him as I drank a cup of stale tea, the bitter taste coating my insides. Nothing looked nice in this house, not even the cups. They were chunky and small, patterned with orange squares. My mother and I had had beautiful things but they were gone, their shadows wrapped neatly in my brain. I couldn't imagine any of them in here, in the house that had been built by Mats' great-grandfather. They didn't fit.

There was nothing to do, so I went for a walk in the woods, the bitter tea-taste lingering in my mouth. It was blueberry season, the ground dark and ripe. I ate, my fingertips blackening. If I had known how, I might have built myself a hut and lived out here. Away from the ugliness of it all.

I was stuffing myself with berries when I found the earring. A silver heart, bejeweled, something Jennie might have worn. It felt good in my palm so I kept it there as I went back to the house. In my room, I put it under the pillow. My fingertips smeared berry juice over the linen.

"Enjoying your stay?" Mats asked when we had our dinner, potatoes fried with onion and cubes of bacon. He leaned far back in his chair, balancing the plate in one hand.

"It's okay." I took small bites, tried to finish my food slowly. Jennie had used to tell me I ate like an animal.

Mats snorted at my reply. "I should've known you'd come back to bother me some day. After the world spit you out."

"It didn't." I remembered the letter the school had sent me in June, misspelling my name in three places. *Dear Carolin, we regret to inform you that...*

"You always were a weird kid, that's what Yvonne said. She told me you didn't have friends. That other kids were afraid of you." Mats shoved food into his mouth without breaking eye contact. His tone was light, as if he were commenting on the weather.

"She was wrong," I said, the lie worming itself into my food, spoiling it. Mats chuckled, and I hated him, and I wanted him to be in the ground instead of my mother.

Dinner was finally coming to an end when he had a call.

"Hey. Oh? Yeah, I'm coming." He hummed to himself as he slipped the phone back into his breast pocket. "I've got to pop out for a while. You stay put, hear?"

As if I were a dog. I nodded, dark thoughts whirling through my head like inverted snow. Mats got into the pickup and left, and I washed the dishes. The house was quiet around me, the air heavy with beer and bacon fat. Once I had been alone a while, I decided to go out and look for more blueberries. Breathe pine air and think about that hut I would never build. It was cool outside, sundown draining the woods of color. I slid past the cars filling the yard, skulked in their shadows like a mouse in a laboratory maze. The woods looked less inviting at this hour, and I thought about getting lost out there. Mats was off somewhere and my phone had no reception. Aimlessly, I walked past the sheds; a toolshed, a workshop, an outhouse, and the garage where Mats had told me he kept his quad bike and an old Cadillac. The deer skulls over the barn doors were small, delicate little faces with no fur or eyeballs left. As I watched them, I heard that puppy whine again. Maybe Mats had a dog? But this one sounded much too small to live outside on its own. The puppy in our building, its name had been Coco. Every time I saw it I wanted to touch that melting-sugar fur, but I never did.

The deer skulls watched me quietly, and I moved toward them. There was a padlock on the barn doors, but it hadn't been properly closed. Maybe some of the furniture from the dollhouse was in there? It was huge, after all, could fit our old apartment ten times over in between its walls.

The barn wrapped me in dust and damp and the smell of mice. The light switch didn't seem to work, so I used the flashlight on my phone. The silvery light was ghostly, running across the cobwebs and wooden beams like a phantom hand. Old furniture was stacked on top of each other next to paint tins and, strangely, my old bicycle. I had no idea why it was here, in a place where I had never been. Dust coated it gray now but it had been blue, and I turned my head so it would stay blue. I tried looking for other things that had been ours, my mother's and mine, but there was nothing. Only the bicycle that shouldn't be there.

Something sparkled on the floorboards, half-hidden behind an armchair. I leaned down and recognized the earring I had found in the woods. A silver heart, a different one, because mine had been whole and this had several jewels missing. It made me sad for some reason. I didn't want it to be on the dirty floor, just like I didn't want my mother to be in the graveyard. I trudged through the barn with the earring clutched in my palm, the light beam from my phone staining the walls.

There was a loft at the far edge of the building, in the darkest corner. The stairs leading to it was little more than a ladder. I hesitated before climbing it, not sure it would hold. Not sure why I was going up there at all. The stairs creaked, and the earring cut into my skin. Puppy whines sullied the air around me, but it could be the wind, too. The more I thought about it, the more certain I became that it was just the wind, the woods, and ancient hinges.

The loft seemed normal at first. Stacks of old newspapers, paperbacks in banana boxes. A navy-blue raincoat on a hanger. I tiptoed across the floor, light beam leading the way. The newspapers were stacked so high that I couldn't see past them.

Then I turned the corner. And I saw it.

Skulls. Skulls, like those over the barn doors—but these were human. Spotless, rounded, ivory white. Four human skulls hung on the wall, with slack jaws and eye sockets that seemed obscenely dark, as if they had been painted black. Underneath them, on an old emigrant trunk, were some other objects. A striped scarf. A pair of glasses. The remnants of a hand.

I scrambled down the stairs, out of the barn. My fingers trembled as I put the padlock back in place. The wind combed through my hair just like my mother had done, and that labored whining trailed around me like a mosquito or persistent fly. I went back inside the house. Put the earring next to its twin and watched them sparkle for a moment before I lowered the pillow. Mats came home an hour later and started watching a noisy soccer game on TV. I stayed in the pink room, watching the horses.

"I bet you're already tired of this place," Mats said the next morning during breakfast. The tea was acidic but I forced myself to drink, swallow.

"Why?"

"There's nothing here. Not for someone like you."

Had my mother known about the skulls? I shoved the thought away because it spawned others, each one nastier than the last.

"Then why are you here?" I asked to cut the bad thoughts down.

"This house has been in my family for generations." Mats stopped buttering his toast for a moment. It was burnt at the edges, as if he'd snatched it out of the fire.

"Yes. Your great-grandfather."

"That's right." He smiled, a sudden grin that was too wide. I wondered if he kept his missing tooth in that loft as well, with the skulls and the shriveled hand.

"My mother didn't like it here," I said. "She can't have."

Mats was quiet for a long while. Melted butter ran from his toast onto the table, but he didn't notice.

"Things were different when Yvonne was around," he said at last. "She bought plants, filled the house with them. *Green fingers*, isn't that what it's called? But they all wilted when she died."

I stayed inside that day, reading books I'd found at the back of the closet in my room. Little-girl stories about dolls and magic, and some handbooks about astrology. Jennie had been obsessed with astrology; had read her horoscope out loud every morning. *You're going to find the one*. As if a girl with looks and friends and money would need a horoscope to tell her that.

Going to bed before ten PM wasn't usually a problem, but that night I had trouble sleeping. I blamed the books, because they had made me think about Jennie. There was no need to think about her anymore; she was on the bathroom floor and wouldn't go anywhere. The whole thing was on my mind, though, because Jennie's mother used to call on weekends and today was Sunday. She had used to ask about me sometimes— *What's it like being roommates? Are you girls getting along*? It was a good thing that she didn't have my number.

It must be nearing midnight when the front door opened. Mats had gone out. Peeking through the blinds, I saw him stride toward the barn. The dead deer stared at him. He slipped inside and light illuminated the barn from inside, outlining each board in the walls. The switch must not have been faulty after all. I put on my jeans and sweater and followed him, ignoring curfew. He might get angry, but I was too curious to care.

The night air was torn by animal sounds, as if starving hounds or carrion birds were out there with their fangs and beaks. I entered the barn noiselessly. My old bike stared at me, back to its true color now that it was swimming in light. Mother-eyed blue. I slid past it, up to the loft where the sounds grew and faded as if a child was toying with the volume button. There was another noise, too, a rhythmic thumping. When I came around the corner I saw Mats, wearing the raincoat. He was standing in front of the emigrant trunk, hitting it over and over with his boot. The things on top of it had been removed and it was open, letting out a stench that reminded me of the dorm room, of Jennie, of the bathroom floor.

I went up to him and looked inside. The girl in there was naked, with her legs strangely bent and dark hair covering her face. Mats stopped kicking the trunk and looked at me.

"You're not supposed to be here, Caroline. You're breaking the rules."

Jennie had used to tell me that whenever I came over to her side of the room. *You're not supposed to be here.*

"Is she going up on the wall?" Now that I knew the sounds came from the girl, they made sense. The realization calmed me.

"She was trespassing," Mats said. "It's just how it is."

I couldn't see what she looked like but I knew she was pretty. Jewel-earring pretty, like Jennie.

"My mother wouldn't like this."

"Well, your mother's been gone a while." His voice was tired, but it was quite late. Almost midnight. "If you're going to stay, you'll have to help me. And if you ever tell a soul, you're going in that trunk yourself, of course."

I nodded. It was reasonable. When he forced her head up I saw that she had Jennie's face, and it made everything so much easier. I would have needed a raincoat of my own, but there was only the one. The girl made sounds until the end, when the floor was slippery wet and my hands the color of canned tomatoes.

"That's enough," Mats said. "I'll handle the rest."

As I headed back toward the stairs, I spotted something on the floor. The hand. Mats was leaning over the girl, preoccupied, so I picked it up. It felt like a dead branch, and the skin was leathery and browned. But I could still read the four-letter word inked on the wrist.

Back inside, I went to my room and pulled away the pillow. The earrings twinkled at me, and Jennie was gone, and there were no animal sounds left because I had put them out. Smiling, I put the earrings on. They were heavy, hurt a little, but it didn't matter. I kept smiling as I closed my eyes and saw those bottle-green walls, the window sill wide enough to curl up on. I would stay forever, never leave. And my mother would live in the dollhouse with me.

Previously published in Nocturne Magazine Issue 2, 2022

AUTHOR NOTE

My first note about this story, then tentatively titled *The Collector*, was written in September 2012: *Daughter reunites with father and discovers that he collects human hair.* For some reason, I didn't write the story until February 2022. *love* is a much crueler tale than *The Collector* was ever meant to be, and a big difference from the original idea is the central role that Caroline's dead mother plays. *love* may be a dark horror story about despicable people, but at its core it's really about sorrow and how it breaks us apart.

Some of my stories are very firmly set in my own rural part of Sweden, and *love* is one of those. Untended yards filled with rusty old cars are no rare sight around here, and something about places like that always piques my interest. The barn in the story is loosely based on the barn at my parents' house, which is crammed with just as much stuff and has a loft like the one Caroline discovers. No human skulls, though (as far as I know).

Wishes

Eliza didn't want to leave but the old woman was angry, screaming about policemen, and there was just no other way. Baby's mouth slithered against her skin as she tumbled out the kitchen window, through the garden, spindly sunflowers tittering. Barberry thorns clawed at her, clawed at Baby, and she hissed at them to stay away.

She sang for Baby like she did at night, that old song, her voice a broken tune. *Hush, little one*. The shawl warmed them both, thick as a bear's hide, gray with streaks of red. It smelled of the place she had come from, the woman with the braids and the cool hands. It smelled like earth and juniper tea.

"We'll find her," she told Baby, who was too small to remember the braided woman and fit beneath the shawl like a small animal, a kitten or a pet mouse. "She can help."

The city was smelly, rough around the edges, and she wished the old woman hadn't found them. The pantry had been dark and there had been nothing but canned peaches to eat, but it had been safe until the woman opened the door and started screaming. Eliza used to make a thorough search before she moved in somewhere, check closets and attics, but now that Baby was with her she was tired all the time, and all she'd wanted was to sink down on that floor and shove sticky, juicy peaches in her mouth. And look where it had got her.

Some men were standing around outside an old storefront down the street, warming their hands over a fire.

The sign above their heads seemed vaguely familiar but half of the letters had been worn down, and she couldn't remember what the shop had sold or if she'd ever gone inside.

"You there, got any food?" The men called out to her, raspy voices, arms reaching out. Eliza pulled the shawl tighter around Baby and sang the song over and over until it became an ocean for the man-voices to drown in. The street helped, showed her alleys and exits. She came into a backyard and the world was quiet around her, like that night when the braided woman had woken her up because it was snowing.

"I haven't seen snow in years," she'd told Eliza. "This is one of those memories you have to keep. So you can tell people about it."

Eliza had looked into the night sky and let the snowflakes fall on her face, into her open mouth. For a long time afterward she thought they were stars, dead stars falling from the sky. And since the braided woman had told her about shooting stars and the wishes they granted, she made a wish every time a tiny crystal landed on her skin.

I want a bed to sleep in.

I want a proper house.

I want Mama and Papa to come back for me.

The memory made her pull a face, nostrils twitching like from a rancid odor.

"It's got nothing to do with us," she told Baby and wrapped the shawl around him, hid him in wool and warmth. "It's in the past."

The backyard was a barren land, all concrete and scrap metal, the sky a square window of moonlight up ahead. There were three doors hanging from their hinges and she asked Baby which one to take, but Baby was sleeping. Eliza tiptoed through the middle door because it was the smallest, and she liked small things. Inside was darkness laced with smells—greasy garbage food, mold, decomposition. She pulled the shawl tight, so tight, around Baby and sang as she moved through the building, sang to keep the wickedness away. When she lived with the braided woman, a stranger came to them one evening, and in the morning they realized that she was sick. But the braided woman had teas for it, teas to make the sickness go away, and when they buried the stranger her face looked almost peaceful. Eliza knew what the sickness looked like but she didn't know how to make the teas and had no kettle, nothing. The braided woman had given her the shawl and sent her off into the world because there were other girls who needed her, or because Baby—

No, it had nothing to do with Baby. She was getting the timeline wrong, that sometimes happened, it was nothing strange. The braided woman had been kind and if Eliza could only find her, she would know what to do.

She escaped the building through a broken window, escaped the corpse-smell and the ghost-howling. The street outside was cold, wintry, and she thought again about her snow-wishes.

She sang to Baby who slept, a doll in her arms, a bundle of skin and coal-dark hair. Rushing down the street was easy, sticking to the shadows was the simplest thing. The braided woman had taught her well. *Don't talk to strangers. Don't let anyone see you. Don't get preg—*

"We'll find her," Eliza whispered into the folds of the shawl. "We'll make her see that she was wrong."

Voices bounced between the abandoned apartment buildings, shrill and laughy. Child voices. Eliza quickened her pace, holding Baby tighter. She had lived with the braided woman for years but she had only rarely been allowed to climb up to the surface, and the tunnels had been hidden well. That night when she'd been kicked out, she'd been so confused and terrified that she'd barely noticed her surroundings.

"But it can't be that hard." Baby's weight was reassuring, an anchor keeping her moored. "She'll have marked the tunnel entrance, because she wants me to come back."

The children laughed again and she ran, jumping over trash piles and debris. She sang to keep Baby from crying, sang to soothe herself. The city closed in on her and she raised her voice until there was nothing but the words that the braided woman had taught her, and the tiny body in her arms. When she collapsed the shawl embraced her, became a world for her to hide in.

She woke up on a mattress and she thought, *one wish granted*.

"Who is she?" someone asked, a young voice, a voice like exhaust fumes and gasoline.

"Scavenger," an older voice replied. "Aren't they all?" *Braids*, Eliza thought, *juniper tea*. She wanted to open her eyes but there was something in the way, a piece of cloth, and ropes digging into her wrists.

Baby, she tried to say, but the word wouldn't come out right and she remembered that the braided woman had teas for that as well. Her tongue was coated with a bitter venom that made her want to be sick, but nothing came.

"They are getting clever," said the gasoline voice, and something ran across Eliza's forehead. A gloved hand. "How long do you think she's been infected?"

"The parasite was still small." The braided woman's voice but still not. "She seems to have thought it was an actual child."

Laughter, tittering. The clang of metal.

Eliza sang quietly, in her head, sang to Baby as wishes flurried through the air and disappeared.

"This won't hurt at all," said that voice from her childhood, the voice that tasted like snow. "Hush, little one."

AUTHOR NOTE

Dystopic fiction is one of my many literary obsessions. I've written quite a few short stories set in post-apocalyptic worlds, and *Wishes* is one of them. Eliza is a lost soul clinging to her baby, the only one she has left. She's eager to get back to the closest thing she's ever had to a home—the place below ground where she lived with a braided woman who was like a mother to her. But her perception of reality is flawed and she can't see anything clearly, not even the truth about the child in her arms. On an unrelated note: I've never had juniper tea, but I'd love to try it.

The idea for *Wishes* came to me from out of nowhere and I wrote it quickly. It's the kind of story that I can't really explain what it's about—it's just there, open for interpretation.

Questions From Between

WRITING

What is your favourite part of the writing process?

I love writing the first draft, but I'm not as fond of editing, simply because I've got so many ideas and I just want to write them all down.

When do you write?

I prefer writing early in the day, but I'll write whenever I have time, really. Never at night, though, since I'm a morning person.

What is the starting point of a story for you? A central idea, a character, a 'feel', even? Or something else?

I've found that many of my ideas need to be connected to another idea before they turn into an actual story, and it can sometimes take years before two ideas are connected like this. One idea can be a character, but then I don't know what that character's story is until another idea pops up and I realize that they could work together. These ideas can be characters, settings, a mental image, or just a story title.

Do you have particular genres within horror, themes, or types of characters that you find yourself coming back to repeatedly in your work?

Horror of the quiet, psychological kind is what I like the most, and most of my stories belong to that subgenre. I'm also very fond of dystopian fiction, and have written several stories set in post-apocalyptic worlds. My stories tend to be about childhood, family, and a loss of innocence, and I love evil characters whose dark side is hidden and doesn't show until it's too late. Morally grey characters and unreliable narrators tend to show up quite often in my writing as well.

Do you plot your stories out beforehand? 'Pants' your way through it? Or some unholy combination?

It depends, so an "unholy combination" might be the best way to describe it, really. I sometimes plan every little thing, and other times I just open a blank Word document and start writing.

Do you approach the writing of short and longer works in the same way, or is there a difference?

There is quite a big difference, I think. The longer the story, the more I need to plan and outline before I start writing. Most of my short stories are based on just a couple of notes, but with some longer stories I've felt the need to plan a bit more.

Do you write these stories in English, or do you draft in Swedish at first?

I usually write directly in English, but some of the stories I've published were first written in Swedish, since I didn't really start writing in English until eight years ago. When I outline a story, my notes tend to be in both languages.

Is it difficult to write in a second language, or does it just come naturally at this point?

It was difficult when I first started, but by now it does come pretty naturally. Of course, there are times when I struggle because my English vocabulary is more limited, but the main problem I've encountered is that it can be difficult to describe things that are specific to my own country and might be confusing to people from other places. Because of that, the world where my stories take place is Sweden, but a sort of alternate version. Though

I should say that I have a couple of stories that are set in other parts of the world as well.

Are you a quick writer? How long (on average) will it take you to complete a short story?

I do think I am, though it depends on who I'm comparing myself with. But a short story usually takes a few days to complete, though there are five-page stories that have taken me years from start to finish...

When it comes to acceptances, do you tend to know which stories will most easily find a home, or does it often come as a surprise?

I do sometimes, but there are stories that have been accepted on the first try that I didn't think were anything special. But of course, I'm more confident about some stories and I will try hard to get them published even though they get rejected repeatedly.

Do you prefer writing short works, or longer?

I honestly can't say I prefer one or the other. I love novel-writing because it allows you to lose yourself in a world you've created and spend a lot of time together with the characters, but I also very much enjoy the precise art of writing a story in just a few pages. There's also the fact that novels take lots of time and effort, and a short story can be completed in a day. That's another reason why I like to write both novels and short fiction.

Do you ever succumb to so-called 'writers block'? How do you get past it?

Yes, it happens now and then and it's always frustrating. I usually get past it by setting up some really simple writing goal, like a hundred words every day, just to get back to where I was and rediscover the joy of writing. Sometimes it helps to write about the writer's block and/or other writing-related problems, instead of pressuring myself to come up with a piece of fiction.

Self-promotion seems to be a big part of an author career these days, are you conscious of having to push yourself out into the world and make yourself seen? Is that something you feel adept at?

Yes, I'm very conscious of that, although I don't feel that I'm particularly good at it. Right now, I'm focusing mostly on my Swedish Instagram account, but I'm constantly nagging myself for not being more active on my international account and on Twitter. I do post something every once in a while, though!

Which part of your writing do you think has strengthened most since you began your writing career?

As a teen and a young adult, I think my writing could be a bit pretentious; I was highly inspired by classic writers and I couldn't imagine writing anything set in modern times. Then, as I got older, I found my style and I realized that I could write contemporary stories just fine. Even though I'll always have a weak spot for historical settings.

Do you have a piece of your own work that you're particularly proud or satisfied with?

I'm satisfied with Lineage that ends my short story collection *Growth*. It's the longest story in the collection and it has been with me for a very long time. I'm very fond of the characters in it even though they are, of course, detestable.

The Lion Game

Hanna doesn't like the Doctor Days. The house smells different then, all sharp and twisty, like the bottles Berta uses for cleaning. The doctor has a big belly, like Santa Claus, but his eyes never look right at her and he has knives in his black bag. She opened it once when he had left it in the hallway and they gleamed at her, big-dog fangs but made of steel. He carries the bag around wherever he goes and Hanna hides from it, from him, from the fangs that like the taste of flesh more than anything. Lydia once told her a story about a wolf whose favorite food was children, but she doesn't remember how it ended. Sometimes things get lost in her head, but she imagines that they are lurking in there somewhere. The children, and the wolf.

"What do you think, Doctor?" It is Lydia's voice, whipped-cream soft, trailing down from the doorway to Mamma's room. "Is she getting better?"

Hanna cowers in the nook behind the stairs where only Grandfather can see her, but he is gone and just a painting on the wall.

"We shall see, Mrs. Alm. Adjust the dosage of the laudanum like we discussed before, and we shall see."

He doesn't take coffee in the drawing room this time, though Berta has baked her lemon sponge and Lydia insists, saying that surely... Instead it's Lydia and Berta at the drawing room table, while Hanna sits on the bench by the window with her glass of raspberry juice.

"Don't spill on your pinafore," Berta says in that voice that is strict but only on the outside, like a crust. "I don't know how many times I've rubbed stains out of it this week."

"He said that the laudanum might be the issue." Lydia holds onto her cup when she speaks, her fingers bony like the twigs under the oak-tree in September. "I don't know what to think. Haven't we tried everything by now?"

Berta bites into a piece of cake, holding the saucer close to her mouth so she won't get any crumbs on the carpet. Her hand is reddish from scrubbing and cooking. "The poor girl."

Lydia nods. Her head looks heavy, balancing on top of her thin neck, with silver hair and a face like mist, pale and hard to see through. "He thinks she'd benefit from professional care. You know what kind."

"I know." A crumb sticks to Berta's upper lip. "What would that look like? Her in a place of that sort?"

"Indeed." Lydia folds her hands in her lap and fixes her eyes on Hanna for a moment that lasts too long. "She is family, and it is our duty to take care of her. No matter what Doctor Berg might think."

Out in the hall the big doors open, *bang*, and there's whispering and laughter and shoes scraping against the floor. Hanna sips her juice, eager to finish it before they enter the drawing room. Christian and Cecilia.

"You started without us?" Cecilia flurries into the room, dimpled and pretty, leaning in to cut a piece of the sponge. Auburn strands of hair have fallen out of her braid, thick and wavy. "I won the match, but don't tell Christian I said so."

"I can hear you, you know." Christian comes after, sleeves rolled up the way Lydia hates, but Christian never cares about Lydia's opinions on anything. "There's coffee, I hope, and not just tea. You know I need my coffee after badminton, Mother."

"Children." Lydia regards them coolly, saying nothing though Christian spills coffee on the table and Cecilia speaks with her mouth full. "Doctor Berg was here."

"Oh, we saw him." Christian scoffs. "That old quack, why won't you tell him to stop bothering us? I don't expect he's doing it for free."

"Amanda isn't getting any better," Cecilia says, "and she doesn't like Doctor Berg. All he does is upset her."

"It is his duty to see to his patients. You should be grateful that your sister is so well looked after."

"Not by him." Cecilia plops down in the armchair by the window, balancing her teacup in one hand and the half-eaten cake in the other. "You're the one doing all the work, Mother."

Christian and Cecilia are allowed to call Lydia *mother*, but Hanna can never call her *grandmother*. Berta has reminded her more than once.

"Work? Taking care of a loved one is hardly work."

Hanna holds her empty glass with both hands, afraid it will fall and break into a thousand pieces on the floor. It happened once and Lydia looked like she would start shouting, but Cecilia said that *we must be nice to the poor little thing*.

"Anyway." Christian is the only one standing, in the center of the room next to the table, like a waiter in a restaurant. Hanna has never been to a restaurant but Cecilia has told her about the music, the candles, and the list of food where you can pick anything you want. "I shall be going out this evening. It might get late."

"Again, Christian?" Lydia's face sags with tiredness for a moment, and Hanna gets a glimpse of the teeth. Her grandmother's teeth, rotting at the back of her mouth.

"Leave the gate unlocked," Christian tells Berta, ignoring Lydia's comment. "But maybe you don't take orders from us anymore, seeing as how my mother treats you like a member of the family."

"Christian!" Lydia's pale eyes widen. Berta fidgets with the hem of her apron, her face turned down as if that would mean Christian couldn't see her.

"We don't have tea with the servants, Mother." He finishes his coffee and leaves, but his shadow seems to stay, white-dressed, slender.

"That boy," Lydia says, and her eyes land on Hanna. The glass turns slippery like an earthworm and Hanna has to squeeze it hard to keep it from falling. "Well, are you done? Then go up to the nursery and play."

Hanna puts her glass on the big table and curtseys, because that's what Berta has taught her. Cecilia winks as if they have a secret together. Hanna likes that thought.

On the stairs she overhears Lydia talking. Her voice trails after Hanna, snake-like, too loud to flee from.

"It would be easier," Lydia says, "if she wasn't such an ugly child."

Hanna has a doll of her own, baby-sized, all curls and frills. It's called Sophianna, which Christian claims is not a name at all, but he can't know all the names in the world even though he's old and reads books so heavy Hanna can barely lift them. With Sophianna clutched in her hand she heads into the garden the next morning, after eating her porridge at the kitchen table. It's Saturday—she knows this because she got a spoonful of jam with the porridge, and a pool of melting butter although she likes it better without. Sophianna doesn't eat but sometimes Hanna makes her, when Berta is busy at the stove.

She stops to admire the peonies outside the kitchen window, cloudy pink like Sophianna's cheeks. Berta has told her not to go anywhere near the flowerbeds, but if she was allowed she'd sit by the peonies all day. She's not, so she has her own secret place.

At the far end of the garden, where the hedge marks the border between the house and the river, Hanna sits down under the oak-tree and puts Sophianna in front of her, leaning against the trunk so she won't fall. Sophianna watches as Hanna reaches into her pocket and takes out her bag of marbles, cerulean like the sky, like river-water and doll-eyes. Carefully she places them in the dewy grass, a circle of blue marbles catching the light, twinkling when she moves her head. Sophianna sits there like a queen and Hanna watches her mouth as if it would start talking if she only waited long enough.

"Hanna?" Berta comes out through the kitchen entrance, rolling pin in hand, face turned toward the river. She knows about the oak-tree, about marbles and dew. "Come inside. Your mother wants to see you."

Hanna runs. She forgets about Sophianna and has to return for her, because Sophianna can't be out in the rain and if Hanna left her outside Lydia would like her even less than she already does.

Mamma's room. Berta holds her hand, drags her up the stairs. Outside the door she takes out the shimmery key, Hanna knows it, has seen it many times.

"I need to go and see to my cookies," Berta says, pulling the door open. "Stay here with your mother until I come back, and don't make her upset."

The room smells sour, like morning breath, but Hanna forgets about that after a while. What does it matter when there are so many things to see—the cat painting, the dressing table, the floral wallpaper. Mamma, sitting up in bed in her white dressing gown, smiling.

"Hanna." Mamma stretches her arms out and Hanna rushes toward her, burying her nose in Mamma's chest. It's not soft like Berta's but she still likes it the best.

"How are you?" Mamma's hair is as auburn as Cecilia's but too short for braiding, and something about it reminds Hanna of the chickens Berta sometimes plucks outside the kitchen door. The feathers dropping to the ground make her sad and Mamma's hair saddens her, too.

"Berta is baking cookies," Hanna says. "With almonds on top."

"Oh." Mamma pats her arm, eyes darting over to the cat painting. "That's good. You like almonds."

Hanna nods. Mamma knows what she likes, even though they don't see each other often. "Can I play at the dressing table?"

"Of course you can." Mamma's smile is thin and barely there, but it is still a smile. Hanna climbs off the bed and walks across to the dressing table, which has three mirrors and too many drawers to count. Sitting down on the white chair, she starts pulling open the drawers, grabbing at pearls and earrings. The three mirror-girls in front of her watch but she doesn't look at them. Doesn't want to see their faces that don't look like they should.

"What's it like outside?" Mamma's voice drifts through the room, mingling with the sound of pearls rattling, drawers being opened and closed. "Is it still summer?"

Hanna puts Mamma's rings on her fingers, piling them on each other since they are much too big to fit. Even though Mamma's hands are almost as skinny as Lydia's. "It's warm," she says, not sure what Mamma wants to hear.

"That's nice. You know, when I was a little girl we used to row down the river on sunny days. I watched my face in the water and they sang for us, Mother and..."

Hanna glances in the right-hand mirror to spy on Mamma. Her head hangs and her shoulders are shaking. The rings rain over the table, *cling, clang*, and Hanna scoops them up and drops them in the right drawer. She doesn't want to play anymore.

A door slams shut somewhere on the same floor, and Mamma twitches.

"Let's go for a walk." It's Cecilia's voice. Cecilia—Hanna wishes she could go to her, sit on her lap like she did when she was younger. Listen to stories from the fairytale book in the nursery.

Mamma lifts her face. Their eyes meet in the mirror but Mamma doesn't seem to know she's there. She's staring ahead, panting, her hands clawing at the bedding.

"Breakfast first," Christian says, they're right outside the door now, Cecilia's heels clacking. "I need my coffee, sister dear."

Mamma starts screaming. No words, just noise, just her mouth wide open and that scream coming out of it, tearing down the wallpaper, the lace curtains, everything. Hanna hides her face and cries, and she keeps her eyes covered as Berta comes rushing in, takes her in her arms and brings her downstairs.

"Don't you worry," Berta says and hands her a cookie fresh from the oven; it's a little burnt and too hot to eat. "She needs some sleep, is all. You know she tires easily."

A while later Lydia enters the kitchen, a chemical whiff about her that makes Hanna's nose itch.

"I thought you said she was manageable today. Cecilia had to help me hold her down."

Berta dries the newly-washed plates but the towel is soaking, dripping onto the floor. Hanna watches the stain of water, the way it reshapes and grows. "She was manageable," Berta says. "They must have done something."

"Berta." Lydia's voice is like the icicles hanging off the roof in winter. "Know your place. You are not to speak out of turn."

Hanna recalls them in the drawing room, clinking china and a tang of raspberry.

"Of course, Mrs. Alm. I apologize."

Lydia's mouth twists into a smile. "No matter. Keep an eye on the girl. I'll handle things upstairs."

Christian is out at luncheon and still hasn't returned when it's time for dinner. Mamma stays in her room as always which saddens Hanna a little, but she can't be sad for long when Cecilia is there, smiling at her from across the table. Then, once dinner is over and they have relocated to the drawing room, Cecilia allows Hanna to stand behind the sofa and brush her hair.

"He has to work now and then," Cecilia says as Hanna draws the heavy silver brush through her locks, enjoying the caress of Cecilia's thick mane over her fingers. "Really, Mother, you should be grateful that he does."

"Working, at this time of night?" Lydia knits, her hands moving frantically while the rest of her body doesn't move at all. "No, I don't think so. Up to his old tricks again, I'm sure."

Berta sits by the window, a pile of socks in her lap. She examines them for holes and tears, head bowed so low that Hanna can spot the bun of tied-up hair at the back of her neck.

"Mother, you have to let go of the past." Cecilia's voice is light, it skips through the air on angel feet. "Everything is fine."

Berta lets out a sound, a laugh of some sort, and Cecilia stands. The brush is torn from Hanna's grip and gets stuck in Cecilia's long hair where it dangles, a streak of silver.

"This only concerns the family, and not you." Cecilia sounds angry and Hanna cowers behind the sofa, watching the heap of socks in Berta's lap. From a distance it looks like a black cat, sleeping, purring softly.

"Cecilia, sit down." Lydia's mouth, it's moving and Hanna sees them though she doesn't want to, the teeth, Lydia's rotten teeth. "You're causing a scene, and I don't see what for."

"She shouldn't think she's any better than us." Cecilia watches Berta who keeps mending the socks, calmly, like she's alone. "We're all in on it. Even her. Do you hear that? You think you're kind, but you're evil. Evil like me, like Mother." She sobs and rushes out of the room, crying, the brush still entangled in her hair.

"I think it's time for the little one to go to bed." Berta stands, putting her pile of mending aside for another day. Hanna hides behind the sofa still, confused by Cecilia's outburst, and sad she didn't get to braid her hair.

"I hope Christian will be back soon." Lydia's knitting grows, gray like her eyes, needles slamming together. "If he comes home drunk Cecilia will have to handle it."

Berta doesn't reply. Upstairs in the nursery, she puts Hanna straight to bed, forgetting about the facewash and the evening prayer.

"Berta," Hanna asks when the lights are out and Berta stands by the door, just about to open it. "Why was Cecilia crying?"

"Good night," Berta says and leaves. Hanna squeezes Sophianna in her arms and shuts her eyes tight against the darkness.

Mrs. Larsson comes by sometimes to help with the laundry. She's a large woman with a dog-face and beady little eyes, and her hands are always blistered. In the afternoon she takes a break in the kitchen with Berta to enjoy some coffee and small talk. Hanna sits on the stairs outside the kitchen door with Sophianna, playing with the gravel, making patterns.

"Oh, this heat." Mrs. Larsson sighs. Through the open door Hanna sees her fanning herself. "It will be the end of me."

"Now, don't say that." Berta's voice is soft. "I can't handle all of Mrs. Alm's laundry on my own."

Mrs. Larsson scoffs. "Some people say that I'm out of my mind to come here, even though she pays well. I bet they think she's running around as she pleases, wreaking havoc. The madwoman."

Hanna's stomach knots. *Madwoman* is a bad word, a word Mrs. Larsson shouldn't be using.

"Oh, no," Berta says. "We've got her under control."

Mrs. Larsson lowers her voice to a whisper. "I've heard that he was a traveler. Circus performer, something of that kind. Vanished into thin air after making her with child."

"She was always a fragile girl. That whole awful business, it was more than she could handle."

"And her father going off on top of it all. You've really not heard from him in all this time?"

Berta purses her lips. "No. As far as Mrs. Alm is concerned, her husband is no more."

"I say, what sort of man abandons his family? But maybe it was more than he could handle, the whole scandal."

"Maybe it was."

"The child, though." Mrs. Larsson seems unaware of Hanna sitting on the stairs, or maybe she doesn't care. "What a pitiful little thing. Mrs. Alm is kind to care for her but really, wouldn't it have been easier to send them away? Both of them?"

Berta finishes her coffee and stands, starts to clear the table. "Mrs. Alm loves all of her children. No one is being sent away, no matter what they've done."

The next time she visits Mamma it rains, water running down the window, distorting the outside view. Mamma sits at the dressing table, painting her cheeks, dousing herself with perfume. Her nightgown has slipped off one shoulder.

"How do I look?" she asks Hanna who is on the bed, putting a new petticoat on Sophianna. "It's a little simple, I know, but we'll buy new things once we're there."

She looks prettier with the makeup on and that girlish shine in her eyes, but Hanna still likes her better when she's sulking in bed. Mamma is saying strange things, things that don't make sense, because even Hanna knows that they can't leave the house.

"I'm going to work," Mamma says in between smearing her mouth with lipstick, red and glossy. "While we're searching for Father. I could learn to cook or clean, or work at a farm perhaps. Would you like that? Living on a farm, with cows and sheep and a kitten of your own?"

Hanna would like a kitten. "A ginger one."

"Yes, a ginger cat for Hanna." Mamma laughs. "There are just some more preparations but after that, sweetheart, after that we'll go down to the train station, and we'll buy the tickets and... You don't have any money, do you?" She turns her face to look at Hanna, the rouge caking on her cheeks, peony pink. "No, you're just a little girl, aren't you? They wouldn't let you have any money of your own. Not until you're older."

Hanna shrugs, rubbing at a smudge on Sophianna's forehead.

"Father slipped coins into my pinafore pocket sometimes, when Christian and Cecilia didn't see. I bought bonbons from the nice old lady at the square, she was always in the same corner, and she liked me. *Little Manda*, she said. *Little Manda likes her sweets.*"

Mamma starts crying. She puts her hands over her face, drags them down, her fingers staining with pink and red. "Then one day Christian found the empty bag in my pocket and told Mother. After that there were no more sweets for me."

Hanna grabs her doll and leaves, tiptoeing across the room. Mamma doesn't seem to notice. In the hallway Berta waits, turning the key in the lock as soon as Hanna has come out.

"Don't listen to anything Miss Amanda says." Berta grabs hold of Sophianna and straightens her clothing, wipes the smudge from her face. "She won't go anywhere, and neither will you."

When Hanna is playing with Sophianna and the marbles under the oak-tree some days later Cecilia comes over to her, a straw hat shading her face. She crouches next to Hanna, cream-colored dress hem pooling around her feet.

"Oh, look at that. You're taking good care of that doll, aren't you?"

Hanna nods, not sure what Cecilia wants but excited that she has come to talk to her.

"We used to play by the oak too when we were children." Cecilia runs her hand over the tree trunk, smiling. "Christian and I had a hiding place up there among the leaves, but Amanda stayed on the ground, sewing for her dollies, singing. We were so quiet and the foliage was thick;

we could stay in hiding for hours. Then, when she least expected it, we stalked down and started chasing her. The lion game, we called it. Father tried to stop it, because Amanda was such a little crybaby, but we were cleverer than he was." Cecilia giggles, picking up a marble. Twirling it between her fingers.

"Maybe Mamma wouldn't be sad anymore," Hanna says, "if you played with her again."

"You're a funny little imp, do you know that?" Cecilia drops the marble to the ground and stands. "Christian will be home soon. You should go inside and wash your face before teatime."

On her way inside Hanna eyes the peonies, wishing she could show Mamma. Poor Mamma, who has to stay in bed and doesn't know if it's summer or spring.

In the hallway Grandfather greets her from his gilded frame and Hanna holds Sophianna up to show him, since no one else is there to see. Grandfather is slim and fair-haired like Christian, but he's got kinder eyes. If he had still been around Hanna might have found coins in her pockets, too.

Christian returns a while later, newspaper tucked under his arm, with smiles and chatter for Lydia and Cecilia. He carries town-smells with him, tobacco and automobile fumes and that sour-sweet tang from the market, all mingling with his aftershave.

"There was an accident outside church last night," he says, smoothing his hair. "Driver lost control of his carriage, little boy got in the way, had his head crushed. Four years old."

Lydia's nostrils flare. "That's awful, Christian."

"Yes, that's what I'm saying." He sips his coffee calmly. "Really, Mother, think what you will of me, but I don't particularly enjoy the deaths of innocent children."

Berta looks over at Hanna, who sits on the rug with her embroidery. "There are children present here, in case you had forgotten."

Christian puts his cup away, turning his eyes briefly in Hanna's direction but not really looking at her. "Oh, yes. My sister's little bastard."

Cecilia snorts, then puts her hand over her mouth. Hanna doesn't know what *bastard* means, but from the way Berta flinches she understands that it's nothing good.

"Let's talk about something else," Lydia says. From her spot on the floor Hanna can see her teeth all too clearly. "How is the business coming along? You know you need only ask if there's anything I can do."

"I don't want your help, Mother." Christian glares and Hanna senses the ripples in the air that mean someone is about to start shouting. But Cecilia puts her hand on Christian's arm and he doesn't speak again.

"It's a fine day." Lydia's smile doesn't look real. "What a blessing it is, the summer."

Berta nods. “A blessing indeed.”

“Play something, Mother,” Cecilia says, her hand on Christian’s arm still. “A dance tune; we could all use something lively.”

“If you insist.” Lydia walks over to the piano in the corner that Hanna had almost forgotten they have, because it’s so rarely used. Chipper music fills the room and Christian rises, taking Cecilia’s hand.

“Get out of the way,” Cecilia tells Hanna as they start dancing, Christian’s hands on Cecilia’s narrow waist, her head leaning against his shoulder. Hanna climbs onto the sofa where Berta sits alone, staring at Christian and Cecilia. Lydia plays faster, the tune growing wild, and Cecilia shrieks as Christian grabs her hands and spins her around. Her braid flies through the air and her mouth is open wide, she’s laughing, she can’t stop.

A scream tears through the music and Lydia stands, the piano lid slamming shut. The scream continues: Mamma’s voice. Hanna presses her hands over her ears but it won’t go away.

“Berta!” Lydia hurries out of the room and Berta follows. Footsteps fill the stairs, the house, but Cecilia sinks down in an armchair and Christian shoves his hands into his pockets.

“They should let her be,” Christian mutters. “Attention-seeker. She can’t stand it when we’re not all fawning over her.”

"Christian." Cecilia nods in Hanna's direction, a weird little smile playing on her lips.

"She was always like that, wasn't she? Prancing around, turning people's heads. Batting her eyelashes to get what she wanted. What did I ever get? A scolding; a beating if I was unlucky. While she sat there pretending to cry."

Hanna doesn't want to stay and listen, but she's too afraid to leave. Upstairs, Mamma is still screaming.

"Oh, I know," Cecilia says. "Father's little darling."

"And Mother refused to see how..." Christian turns his eyes to the doorway as if he's expecting someone to stand there listening in. "God, I'm so tired of it all. The pretense, I'm sick of it."

"You don't think I'm tired?"

Christian laughs at this. "If only Mother would learn to play by the rules. That damned doctor she keeps bringing here, what if Amanda starts blabbering to him?"

"You've done nothing wrong. Not really. I don't think any of us have." Cecilia leans back. There's something wilted about her face, like the peonies when they die. "Things go too far sometimes. There's nothing to be done about it now."

"Well, I had to do something. Mother was too blind to see what was going on. It was up to me to set things straight."

Hanna watches Christian's face, wondering what he's talking about. Why he sounds so angry. Suddenly he stares right at her, as if he wasn't aware of her presence until now.

"What is she doing here?" He points at Hanna who shrinks under his gaze, wishing she could become invisible. "Every time I see her all I can think of is—"

"She's Amanda's child."

"And the circus boy's." Christian paces the floor, round and round on the rug where they danced, he and Cecilia.

"Yes." Cecilia stands. She walks over to him and grabs his hand to stop him in his tracks. "Now, try to pull yourself together. We're not children anymore. We have to handle things like adults do."

"We were playing." Christian pulls his hand free from her grip and stares at her. "It was just a game."

"Oh, I know." Cecilia leans in, patting his back.

"I can't breathe in here. I'm suffocating. And that maid, she knows too much."

"What do we care about her? She's no one. Go outside now, have some fresh air to calm yourself. Mother will be very disappointed if you're not present at dinner."

He grabs an empty cup off the table, hurling it into the wall. "I don't give a damn about dinner."

Lydia comes into the room. Calmly she starts picking up the remnants of the cup, the leaf-thin shards. "She's better now. Berta is staying with her until she falls asleep."

"Good." Cecilia grins. "What would we do without Berta?"

Lydia catches Hanna watching her and her expression changes, like the garden outside when it's distorted by rain. "Stop looking at me!" she hisses. "What do you want me to do?"

Hanna wishes Sophianna was there, but she's in the nursery upstairs with the rest of Hanna's toys, the marbles and picture books.

"Mother, you need to sit down." Cecilia's voice is worn, frayed at the edges. "Things are the way they are. We can't change anything."

"It would have been better if she had never been born," Lydia says and Hanna doesn't know if she's talking about her or Mamma, or both. "There was something with her, always something."

"And she was too pretty", Christian says, staring out of the window at the flowerbeds outside, the blossoming peonies. "She only had herself to blame."

Hanna wakes early the next day, when the sky burns over the rooftops.

"We have to help Mamma," she whispers to Sophianna before leaving the nursery and tiptoeing down the stairs. It's spooky when the grownups are all asleep but Grandfather is there on the wall, smiling at her as if he knows what she's about to do.

The gravel stings her bare feet, but it can't be helped. She needs a peony, because it will make Mamma remember that it's summer outside and that there are beautiful things out there in the world, like rivers and flowers and ginger kittens. They have to leave the house and go away, just the two of them. To the train station—that's what Mamma said. As long as they're together, it will all work out somehow.

She needs a pair of scissors to cut the flower, but she's spent many hours in the kitchen and knows where everything is. Like Berta's apron, hanging on a nail behind the door, with the keyring hidden in the front pocket. The keyring Berta uses to unlock Mamma's door.

Hanna sneaks back upstairs, pressing the peony to her chest. It takes a while to unlock the door but she manages in the end, stealing into Mamma's room and shutting the door. It's dusky in there, and the smell makes her bury her nose in the flower.

"Mamma!" She tugs at the quilt. "Mamma, we can go now."

"Stop it." Mamma whimpers, thrashing between the covers. "You can't, you can't. Please stop."

Hanna climbs up on the bed together with Sophianna, carefully placing the peony next to Mamma on the pillow. "Mamma, look! It's summer, so we don't need to bring a lot of clothes. We can go outside right now and pick some more flowers, and then we can go to the train station."

"Go away!" Mamma lashes out with her arm, pushing Sophianna into the floor. There's a thud, but not just that—a crack, too, like when Christian threw the cup into the wall.

Mamma sits up. Starts shaking her. "I said, go away!"

Hanna is only dimly aware of the door bursting open. Footsteps, voices. Someone tearing her from the bed and Sophianna lying there, face split in two, a gash where her mouth used to be.

"The damn kid," someone is shouting. Christian.

"She's always causing trouble." Cecilia. And Berta holding her, squeezing her arms, muttering that she's ungrateful.

"Don't kill him," Mamma wails, squirming, tearing at her nightgown. "You can't do it, you can't."

"Well, what are you waiting for?" Lydia glares at Berta, her face all lines and shade but Hanna only sees her teeth, broken, rotten inside and out. "Get her out of here! I don't want to see her." She snatches the peony off the bed and holds it up for Berta to see. "And this, did you tell her she could pick them? I've told you I don't want them inside the house. I've told you."

Christian and Cecilia glance at each other, smiling as if they're both thinking of the same joke. "Oh, Mother," Cecilia says, picking broken-faced Sophianna up and rocking her in her arms like a baby. "You have to let it go."

"It was the perfect spot." Christian grimaces as Mamma's screams grow louder. "And we dug deep."

"You ruined everything," Lydia says, the look in her eyes reminding Hanna of the story about the wolf. The devoured children. "Now, hold her down. And for the last time, get that cursed child out of my sight."

"You've done it now." Berta leaves the room and drops Hanna on the hallway floor, putting her hands in her sides. Her eyes are almost as mean as Lydia's. "Stole my keys, too, didn't you? You wicked girl. It's only right what happened to your doll. Get out of our way now, and don't try to upset your mother again."

She heads back into the room and shuts the door. Mamma is still screaming in there and Hanna hates it, hates her, all of them. When she sits down at the bottom of the stairs Grandfather winks at her as if he knows a secret, and he wants to tell it to her, too. But portraits can't talk, no matter how life-like they are. He's probably somewhere out there in the world outside, farming, petting a ginger cat. But Mamma will never go there, and neither will Hanna. They wouldn't even let her outside the gate.

Doctor Berg and his black bag come to visit some hours later. Hanna still cowers under the stairs, her little head brimful of knives, Grandfather watching over her. No one has come looking for her or offering her something to eat. After spending the longest time in Mamma's room the doctor comes back out and speaks with Lydia who stands there rigid, lips pursed, teeth concealed.

"My advice is to give her professional care, as I've said before. These institutions, I'm sure you've heard stories about them, but it's not half as bad as that. She'd be well looked after. With luck, she could be out of there in a year or two, fully cured."

"I'm not sending my daughter away, Doctor." Lydia leads the way downstairs, walking slowly, firmly gripping the banister. "What sort of monster would I be if I did that?"

"Ah, and there's the child." Doctor Berg is looking right at Hanna, halting on the stairs, gazing down. *The bag*, is all she can think. *The knives*. "It's a bit of a pity about... Well, she might grow out of it. Either way, it's more important to be good-natured than to have a pretty face."

"Yes." Lydia stares at her as if she'd forgotten about her existence. In her left hand is the peony, crumpled, petals staining the carpeted stairs. "The child."

Hanna darts out of the house. She's barefoot, the gravel stinging her feet, but she doesn't care. She runs through the garden, past the flowerbeds, down to the oak-tree. It's a giant towering over her but she's not afraid, would never be afraid of her oak.

The first few times she tries to climb it she slips, tumbling into the grass and staining her pinafore. It doesn't matter; no one's out looking for her anyway. Then she gets the hang of it, her feet finding the right spots, her arms pulling her upward. She climbs high, doesn't stop until she's hidden among the leaves. It smells good up there, an earthy scent that cradles her the way Mamma should, if Mamma wasn't sick all the time. The leaves tickle her face and she laughs, leaning against the trunk, enjoying invisibility.

Maybe they'll come looking for her soon. Lydia, Berta, Cecilia, and Christian. Pretending they like her, just like they pretend to like Mamma. Pretending everything is as it should, when everything is wrong and always has been.

Hanna will wait for them. She'll wait until it gets dark if she has to, she'll go without food and drink. They're bound to come to the oak-tree eventually. Calling her name, they're bound to come.

And when they do, they'll be very sorry.

AUTHOR NOTE

The first version of *The Lion Game* was written in Swedish in 2011 and called *The One Who Opens the Gate (Den som öppnar grinden)*. I rarely plan my short stories in that much detail, but there are excessive notes about this one. I had also written another story about the characters Lydia and Berta (originally named Gerda) in 2008. *The Lion Game* follows the little girl Hanna, living in the shadow of the past, barely tolerated by a family that doesn't want her. Her mother is confined to her bed, too sick and frail for parenting, and Hanna is left to her own devices or grudgingly taken care of by the maid. Something bad has happened in the house but she doesn't know what it is. All she knows is that it has something to do with her and her mother. *The Lion Game* is one of the short stories I have struggled with the most. Writing child protagonists can be hard, especially when they are as young as Hanna. She is too innocent to realize what is going on around her, but still has to grasp enough for the reader to be able to put things together. For a while I toyed with the idea of making Cecilia the protagonist instead, but no—I wanted this to be Hanna's story. *The Lion Game* is quiet, subtle horror without even a drop of blood, but I think that kind of story is sometimes the scariest of all. Just a small child, surrounded by family but still so utterly alone.

This story takes place in a Swedish small town in the 1910s, a setting that was heavily inspired by the works of Astrid Lindgren, Sweden's most beloved author of children's books. I've always enjoyed historical fiction, and as a horror writer I'm fascinated by the clash between idyllic settings and sinister plots.

Scar

Ravens circling the tower room. Hundreds of raven eyes. The voices rise with every strand touching the floor, every golden lock.

Hair that will grow no more.

Nine years earlier, she sits quietly in the throne room with interlaced hands. The back of the chair points up into the canopied ceiling; she has to stand up on the seat to be able to admire the snow crystals carved into the wood. Now, with so many people present, Princess Stella naturally does no such thing.

The music is loud, but not loud enough to drown out the heavy thuds from beneath the table. Stella doesn't have to look to see Lune and Leal kicking each other's shins. Boys are like that, that's what Ganda says. They can never stay calm for long. Stella's little feet are hidden under the hem of her dress, motionless like she has been taught. She knows better than to start a fight, and even though Lune sits right by her side he has never so much as pinched her. Stella is different. The brothers are protective; they wouldn't harm her. Not even Luc, whose temper is so frightful in the mornings that people stay out of his way. She is the princess of Debre, the only one. Loved and admired by all.

The piper has long red braids and leather shoes in that same fiery shade. Even Stella can guess what the look means, the one that Leo gives the girl. He just turned fourteen; in the kitchen, the maids titter about long, prying fingers while Stella hides under the table with the cat. When she looks out of her window before bedtime, she sees Leo in the courtyard with his sword and his guns. His blows are fast, and his shots never miss the target. Stella doesn't have to be afraid of anything, as long as Leo is around.

The boy beating the drum is pretty, his hands adorned with rings, but Lantos has eyes for no one but Sabir. It is as it has always been. Mother speaks about wedding plans, and Stella looks forward to grand feasts and new clothing. The happiness on her eldest brother's face. It is the wedding they're all waiting for, and after that there will be four others until it's Stella's turn. At night, Ganda tells her about Maris and the white city. About the Glass Palace and the rulers there. When Stella grows up she will be the queen of Maris—Mother has promised her that. She is five years old. She knows exactly what the future holds.

Nine years later, when she recalls the music filling the throne room that day, she doesn't know if she heard it before the scar, or after.

Maybe she was still like she was supposed to be.

To Ganda there is no scar.

"Bow your head, your highness, so we can rinse all the soap out."

Stella's neck is thin and beautifully rounded. All the little ladies of the court want one that is just the same—sometimes, when she thinks they deserve it, she allows them to touch it. Ganda scrubs her hair clean with hard, red hands. The water is hot but Stella cowers in the tub, because there's a gap under the window and it is drafty and cold in the mountains of Debre. Her chamber is never warm, not even in the summer when the apple trees down in the valley bloom.

"Her majesty picked out a dress," Ganda says. Of course, Stella has already seen it. Purple velvet, shoes in the same fabric, the bodice embroidered with golden roses. Royal colors that go with her hair. Her mother has said that it shines brighter than the sun.

"It is wonderful, Ganda."

"Quite so, your highness." Ganda drapes the linen cloth around her thin shoulders and Stella stands, climbing out of the cooling water and onto the floor. Her hair is a large, heavy bundle wrapped up on top of her head, her body as white as milk.

"That's good, your highness. Now put the chemise on." Ganda's movements are slow, and her fingers clumsy as they pull at Stella's silk stockings.

No, Ganda never sees any scar.

The queen of Debre has five sons. They are tall, fair-haired; they will be able to defend the kingdom, should they have to. The counsellors praise Lantos for his sharp mind, his solemnity. Every soldier in the country is looking forward to being led by Prince Leo in the future, or his brother Luc. And at the university in Riza, the scholars are eagerly awaiting Lune and Leal.

But Queen Adrisa only has one daughter. *How lucky*, the ladies of the court whisper to each other. *At her age, she wouldn't have had another chance*. The queen of Debre showers her princess with gold and jewels, pays the finest singers and artists to tutor her, and gives her kittens and whining puppies that are gone without a trace a few weeks later. The queen powders her daughter's cheeks until they glow, and plucks her eyebrows until Stella learns to endure the pain. In the throne room, Stella sits at her mother's feet while the ladies of the court amuse them with their gossip, while they flatter the queen and compliment Stella's new emerald bracelet. Her father is tired and weighed down by duties; she rarely sees him. Occasionally she gets a pat on her head before dinner, never more. To him Lantos is important, Lantos and the four other brothers. But to the queen, Stella is the most important and most beautiful of all.

Through her mother, Stella becomes familiar with the distant Maris. The neighboring kingdom by the great sea, where the rulers travel down paved streets in carriages pulled by white horses. Where lanterns light up parks and gardens, and no one is ever cold. In Maris, Stella's mother claims, even the maids wear silk and powder their hair. In Maris, the ruler's wife doesn't have to sit around in dusky halls, bored out of her wits, because her husband values tradition over comfort and because her country is removed from the rest of the world.

The successor in the Glass Palace is a boy her own age, pale, as dark-eyed as Sabir. Queen Adrisa has met him.

"You will be a beautiful queen one day. That boy will love you. Everyone will love you."

Stella smiles as her mother caresses her cheek, knowing that she will be a queen just like her. Her dreams dance around the Glass Palace in Alba. The light and the masquerades and the constant warmth.

She is ten years old, and she doesn't know what rulers want. What men want.

The woods are deep around the castle in Debre. The five princes spur their steeds on there, draw their bows and lift spears, hunt like their ancestors. At dusk they return, the servants kneeling under the weight of their kills. The ravens follow them.

Princess Stella only visits the woods during summer. That's when she's given permission to go there with her little ladies in waiting, skip along the narrow paths and pick wild flowers. The women stay cooped up in the carriages, watching every step. Stella hears strange birds chirping in the trees and accepts the other girls' sloppy bouquets with the patronizing smile she uses only with them. They are the daughters of courtiers and counsellors, chamberlains and duchesses. They're all hoping to become her confidante, her closest companion.

Stella loathes them.

Still, she thinks Aurelia's flowers are the least ugly, and Aurelia's laughter is the one that hurts her head the least. Aurelia is the child of one of the queen's best friends; she has frizzy brown hair and dimpled cheeks. When Aurelia talks, Stella almost finds it enjoyable.

"My mother visited the masquerade once in her youth," Aurelia says when they are twelve years old and the moss dampens their silk shoes. The foliage overhead weaves itself into a quilt that hides them from the mountains, the clouds, the castle. "She says that there is no city in the world as wonderful as Alba."

It annoys Stella a little to hear someone else speak about the city that belongs to her. That will belong to her.

"My mother the queen has been to the masquerade many times." She doesn't need to say more, to put Aurelia in her place.

"Her majesty was the most beautiful woman in the room, I'm sure," Aurelia grovels and Stella finds it unnecessary to point out that the annual masquerade in Alba is a grand event, that hardly takes place in only one room.

"But your highness will grow up to become even more beautiful, if I may say so." Aurelia's eyes are big. The violets are already wilting in her hand.

"No one can be more beautiful than my mother, Aurelia."

The other girl blushes. When she speaks again her voice is lower, worn thin. "Forgive me, your highness. Please, your highness mustn't misunderstand."

Stella waves her hand. *It's fine. You are forgiven.*

"I would so love it if your highness brought me along to the Glass Palace in Maris. When your highness becomes queen."

Sometimes Stella wonders if she has a friend in Aurelia. She had thought that friendship would feel differently.

Stella watches as her brothers grow. Even Lune becomes long-legged and strong, gets a deep voice and a new decisiveness in his eyes. While the king's hands tremble too much to hold a sword, while his gaze clouds over, Lantos speaks to the counsellors and makes alliances with the leaders in the north. The queen's eyes are wet, and Stella knows that her father is dying.

Stella watches as her brothers grow, but she herself doesn't change. She is a piece of jewelry, a doll to dress up in silk. Even the men in the royal guard must smile when she patters across the courtyard. Queen Adrisa buys pearls and lace gloves for her daughter and Ganda styles her fair hair with combs, ribbons, pins, and bows. Stella watches her own face in the mirror and knows that she is pretty.

A pretty doll with dreams of Alba.

Princess Stella is thirteen years old when the king of Debre dies. They won't allow her to watch when the funeral pyre is lit.

The wedding day she's been waiting for finally comes. Lantos takes Sabir's hand in the crammed royal chapel, and Stella cheers along with everyone else. Around her ankles billow the hems of ten petticoats, and her belly is heavy with pastries. At her side, Aurelia claps her hands together hard.

They lean out from the balcony afterwards, watching the party below. Stella sees her mother smile. They are dressed in the same colors, her mother has arranged it so and everyone, not just Aurelia, has complimented Stella on her gown. The other girl's dress is not half as beautiful, naturally, but still Stella wishes she had been the one wearing it. Having the body it conceals. Aurelia's hips are rounded and soft, just like her developing breasts. There is nothing rounded about Stella. Every morning Ganda laces her tight, so tight, and when she passes a mirror she can sometimes fool herself into believing that she sees something, buds beginning to grow. But without lacing and mirrors, there is nothing there.

"Luc is so handsome. Mother says he puts the poor maids in trouble, what do you think that means?" Aurelia giggles. They are older now, and she doesn't address Stella as formally as she should. Stella knows she has the right to be annoyed by it, but finds she doesn't care.

"I don't know," she lies. Aurelia should know better than to talk about Prince Luc like that.

"Either way, I think he's terribly good-looking. Leal, too, but everyone knows he already has a girl."

Stella doesn't have anything to say about gossip regarding her brothers. Her eyes follow faces, smiles, voices. People moving down there, alone or in pairs. There are a few delegates from Maris, slender black-eyed women draped in gossamer fabrics. No successor, no young ruler's son from Alba.

"Who would you... Stella, if one of the men down there would ask you for a dance. Who would you want it to be?"

People, alone or in pairs. Faces. Stella tries to imagine that one of the men in the room would touch her, and all she can think is that she doesn't know. She can't know.

"You have no right to ask such intimate questions," she snaps at Aurelia who turns flushed and repentant. They fall silent, turn their gazes back to the feast below.

The question stays in Stella's head.

In the night, when Ganda has combed the powder and finery from her hair, Stella is roused from wine and doesn't want to sleep.

"They are a handsome couple."

Ganda merely chuckles. She has listened for hours to Stella's chatter about the dance, the food, the music.

"It's a shame that they can't have any children together."

"Oh, your highness, there will be children all right." Ganda's voice is calm, but Stella knows her well enough to hear that she's tired and eager to go to bed. "The king will father a successor, who will be brought up as the child of him and his consort. After that they can have as many foster children as they please, as long as there is a successor to the throne."

Stella lifts her arms and feels the nightgown run cool and soft over her flat chest. "I'm going to have many children," she says. "At least five."

Ganda nods, tucking her in. "Yes, your highness." She doesn't look at Stella when she speaks.

She breathes in the knowledge, slowly, like ashes and poisonous fumes.

On the night before Yule they bathe in the throne room, the men of the royal family. Lantos and Sabir, and the four other brothers. The page boys carry scorching water up the stairs, filling the tubs. It's a night when no women are allowed.

Is that why Stella lingers in the doorway? Why she spots Lune standing there, his hair damp around his shoulders, before Sabir slams the door shut and the men erupt with laughter.

He looks like her. That's all she can think about, up in her tower room with the wind slipping through. Underneath the cloak and flowing tunic, underneath the bodice and petticoats, they are the same. There's only one place where he's different, beautiful Lune with his lute and his poems.

A place, where Stella has nothing but a scar.

Stella sits straight-backed on her throne. She has become tall now, able to see the snow crystals by simply turning her head. Except for her height, nothing much has changed.

They say that the girl down in the village is walking around with a big belly already. That soon, Lantos will have his firstborn in his arms. He's in the seat of honor; Sabir has taken their mother's place by the king's side. At night, Queen Adrisa strokes her only daughter's head. They talk about the white city, about Alba, about the Glass Palace. About the life Stella will have there.

"I remember it so well," Ganda says often. "Her majesty desperately wanted a daughter. And then she finally had one."

Princess Stella sleeps alone. Lantos and Sabir lie in bed cradling their newborn twins; Leo never lacks bedfellows. Luc divides his attention evenly between the young maids, and Leal has his black-haired lady of the court. It is common knowledge that Lune's page shares his master's bed.

But Stella sleeps alone.

The castle in Debre was built to withstand attacks. The cliffs are in line with the towers, concealing them, and from the highest point of the northern wall you stare down into an abyss. No enemy armies can storm the castle from the north.

The wind blows hard, pushing against their bodies. The five princes are dressed in black leather boots and fur-brimmed cloaks; heavy swords hang from their belts as they ride out into the woods or practice the art of battle in the courtyard. But the princess shivers in thin silk slippers, and her cape isn't trimmed with anything but lace.

The brothers go to bed with maids and page boys. Stella shudders between freezing sheets.

They are men, courageous, strong. She is just a scar, red and rosy between hairless legs.

The little ladies of the court play the harp and recite poetry, perched up on cushions in her chamber. Some are petite, others round-cheeked or skinny. But they all have breasts now, and they complain about stomach pains and flowing blood once a month.

Everyone except Stella.

She prefers when it's just Aurelia and her, though she'd never admit to it. Aurelia doesn't talk as much about boys anymore, and she readily lends Stella any ribbon or jewelry she asks for.

Stella thinks that she might want to bring Aurelia with her to Maris after all.

Together with her mother the queen she talks about the future.

"I'm going to have a hundred white horses."

Her mother smiles, patting her hand.

"I'll have new clothing every day and ten chambermaids waiting on me." Stella has been raised to have big dreams.

"Of course you will, my darling. And no one in Alba will be able to resist you."

Stella loves hearing her mother's flattering. She needs it. Yes, she is pretty, with her flowing locks and dark smudges accentuating her eyes. But Stella turns away from the mirror in the mornings, before Ganda has laced and dressed and brushed and painted. She doesn't want to see the bottom layer.

"Lantos will go to Maris to see the ruler in a few weeks. He will hand over your portrait."

Stella looks up at her mother. She doesn't dare to ask why Queen Adrisa is crying.

The knowledge grows when nothing else does.

Leo comes home drunk one night. People talk about bad company, but Lantos is the one who must decide, and Lantos does nothing. Brothers look after each other. Stella has been fourteen for a long time this night when her brother staggers into the hall. She has no idea why he locks his eyes on her.

"Little Stella." Grave eyes follow him; everyone is gathered. Everyone is there to witness her humiliation. Leo is strong, and she gasps when he grabs her shoulders.

"Tell me, baby sister, why are women so..." He frowns, clearly struggling to find the words. "So damn false, every single one of them."

"Let her go, Leo." Lantos' face is stern. Out of the corner of her eye Stella sees her mother murmur something to herself, words she can't hear.

"You need to eat more," Leo says, giving her poorly padded chest a hard tap. "Can't go around looking like this if you want to get married." He laughs before leaving her. A joke, Stella tries to tell herself. A joke, and he's drunk, and it means nothing. But on the other side of the table her mother's face is ghostly white.

Stella is beginning to wish that Ganda would let her dress herself. She's ugly; she knows that now. The chambermaid shuffles around on heavy feet, puts away gowns and brings out new ones. Seals the gap under the window when the wind howls outside, seals it with the same padding she uses for Stella's fake bosom.

"Ganda," Stella says in the spring when Lantos' twin boys are laughing out in the courtyard. "Why do I have a scar?"

Ganda stands with her back bowed, turned away. Maybe that's why Stella dares to ask. "Scar, what's that supposed to mean? My, your highness looks just like everyone else."

"Lune doesn't have a scar. None of them do."

"It's not proper to talk about such things, your highness. Girls are different from boys." Ganda still hasn't turned around. She has picked the stockings out of the drawer like she was supposed to, but she hasn't turned around.

"I'm not like the girls either." The words stay there, a sharp tone in the air, heavy with accusation. Stella is cold; winter melted away weeks ago but she is cold.

"Well," Ganda says a little bit unkindly before coming over, carrying the stockings in her hand. "Your highness needs to speak to her majesty about that."

Stella knows that she should, but she's not sure if she dares. She thinks about the portrait, her own portrait that Lantos has left in Alba. She remembers her mother's tears.

One night she climbs up to the northern wall and senses the depths under her feet, as the birds cry around her. She's half, she knows that's how it is.

She's not like she's supposed to be.

Aurelia makes it a habit to stay after the other girls have left the princess's bedchamber for the night. Sometimes she's the one who untangles Stella's hair.

Stella doesn't hear any news from Maris. She keeps that dream hidden deep inside. Rulers want curvy girls, or boys with broad shoulders. Rulers don't want scars.

Queen Adrisa rarely leaves her chamber anymore. Stella asks if she can see her and they tell her that she's ailing, that she doesn't have the strength to speak.

They whisper that she won't survive.

Stella overhears Lantos talk with Sabir about the queen. She is overcome by regret, he says. She wants his forgiveness for something, but refuses to tell him what it is.

"She's delirious," Lantos says, unaware that others can hear. "She's rambling about Stella."

Stella sees him slink into the queen's bedchamber at night a week later, and she knows that her mother is about to die. That Lantos will find out the truth.

It might be because Aurelia notices her tears that she follows Stella into the bedchamber that night.

"I want you to cut my hair," Stella says. There's a pair of silver scissors in the box on the nightstand; Ganda uses them sometimes. Aurelia's eyes go wide.

"Can I? Only a little, surely?"

Stella just nods. She's curled up on the bed, sensing Aurelia moving behind her. Braids and pearls and ribbons need to be removed before anything can be cut.

"You can cry as much as you want," Aurelia says as the brush scratches Stella's scalp. "I mean, if you'd like."

"Thank you." Stella wonders if the queen has taken her final breath yet. If she's brought her lips to Lantos' ear and told him the thing that everyone will soon find out about.

That the rulers in Alba will find out about.

"This gown is so cute." Aurelia pinches the fabric, giggling. "Violet really suits you."

Stella could say that violet suits Aurelia, too, because it does. And Aurelia has been kind to her. She has always been kind to her.

I've got something to tell you.

"Now I'm ready to start cutting."

Stella moves over to the window, and Aurelia grabs the scissors.

I'm not a girl.

"How much should I take?"

Stella holds her hand up, lets it brush over her shoulder. Like Lune. Just the same length as Lune. Aurelia stares aghast, then starts laughing.

"Oh, you almost fooled me there! Good heavens, what would people have said?"

Stella just smiles as Aurelia snips off the ends of her curls. As if it would make any difference. She cuts, talks. Once she's finished Stella feels her round arms around her waist for just a moment. Aurelia, who likes her although she isn't like she's supposed to be. Who is warm and cares for her.

"You look nice," Aurelia says before pulling away. "Really nice." Stella takes the scissors to put them back in the box. The floor is strewn with golden hairs, and distant bird cries scatter the air outside the window. She walks across the stone floor, her feet bare. Puts the scissors down beside her but hasn't had time to open the box when Aurelia speaks.

"If you'd like..." Aurelia stands next to her all of a sudden. Her cheeks glow like winter apples. "I could sleep in here tonight." *If you'd like.*

"Because it gets so cold," she adds, speaking fast. "And you might not want to be alone right now."

Stella thinks that Lantos probably knows by now. But Aurelia doesn't know, and she likes Stella and wants to sleep beside her. No one has ever wanted that.

"You can sleep here," she says. Aurelia has to help with her lacings, because Ganda isn't there. Ganda, who has always known. The gown falls to the floor, heavy, lifeless. The chemise, the stockings, and Stella's heart beats madly. Aurelia likes her. Aurelia will keep liking her.

"You're laced so tight." Aurelia giggles as her bodice is removed; Stella is down to her final petticoat. When she turns around, it takes Aurelia a while to regain her bearings.

"Some girls have to wait forever for them to grow, I've heard." She pats Stella's arm. "Don't worry about it." Yes. Aurelia will keep liking her.

The petticoat slips easily off Stella's narrow hips. Ganda has taken it in at the waist several times.

A scar. That is her truth, the only one she has. And Aurelia screams.

"What is that?" She backs away, fumbling at the bed for support. "What are you?"

Stella wants to ask her to be quiet, but no sounds come out of her throat. She is a body, nothing but a scarred body. And Aurelia doesn't like her at all.

"Get away from me!" She hits, aims kicks at Stella. Tears at her hair, the curls that she's always admired. Stella leans over her, trying to calm her down. All she wants is to shut her up. They will hear, they will rush up the stairs, and they will see her. Aurelia mustn't scream.

It happens after that, she's not sure how. The scissors, they gleam in her hand, over and over until Aurelia isn't screaming anymore.

Stella climbs down onto the floor. Blood dribbles from the scissors, pooling darkly at her feet. She's naked, but she isn't cold anymore. Outside the window, the ravens have started to gather.

I've got something to tell you.

The scissors are sticky, but she doesn't let them stop. The birds cry. The birds see. Princess Stella's portrait, hanging on a wall in the Glass Palace in Alba.

I'm not a girl.

Her locks spill to the floor. Around her head they are soon shorter than Lune's, shorter than Leo's. The scissors tickle her neck and ears, tendons and skin. Follow the shape of her head. Stella cuts without stopping. Her hair is gone, but she's not stopping.

I am nothing.

Raven's wings are flapping against the window. At the bottom of the stairs footsteps echo, multiply. Stella cuts, refusing to stop. Like the rough hands that time, when Queen Adrisa decided that she would have a daughter.

The scissors are still moving. Princess Stella's eyes are closed.

I am nothing.

I am a scar.

Previously published in Black Apples, Belladonna Publishing, 2014

AUTHOR NOTE

Scar was originally written in Swedish in 2012 (*Ärr*) and published in the dark fairytale anthology *Black Apples* in 2014. The translation was made by the publisher, but this time the translation is made by me. I think *Scar* is one of the saddest stories I've ever written. Princess Stella certainly didn't get a happy ending to her fairytale.

Set in the fictional kingdom Debre, *Scar* is one of my few fantasy tales. I had written about Stella's world before, in a story called *The Glass Palace*, which is about the place that Stella dreams about: Alba, the white city, and its grand annual masquerade. As a princess, Stella has spent her entire life playing a role, doing exactly what is expected of her. She has been taught that her purpose is to become a queen in Maris, the distant country that is so much nobler and more beautiful than the Debre she has grown up in. When she realizes that her whole existence is based on a lie, her world crumbles. All she has left is her best friend, Aurelia, who will surely keep loving her no matter what—but not even Aurelia accepts her for who she really is beyond her makeup and fancy gowns.

In *Scar*, there is a lot of focus on beauty, fashion, and jewelry, because Stella's life revolves around these things. She has little in common with her five brothers, who are expected to fight and hunt. There are rules to live by, lines she cannot cross—and when she finds out she's not like the other girls, it's too much for her to handle.

Questions From Between

MORE

You have a novel published and suddenly find yourself touted as the new Stephen King, what's the first thing you spend some of that next, meaty advance cheque on??

We recently bought a house, so if I had some extra money I'd probably spend it on something terribly boring but necessary, like installing new windows.

Is there a genre you've yet to fully tackle that you could see yourself writing one day?

I really like classic whodunnits, and it would be fun to try creating a story like that one day. Even though I think I'd be awful at it.

Would you be interested in adapting any of your work for the screen? And is there a particular story or two of your own that you think would be ideal movies?

That's every writer's dream, isn't it? I think the story Lineage from my collection *Growth* would work perfectly as a movie, and I'd love to watch it.

Looking back, is there anything you'd do differently if starting your writing career over?

I wish I would have done things much sooner, because I feel like I wasted many years doing nothing. I spent a lot of time doubting whether I would ever get my stories published, since the few Swedish publishers who accepted individual short stories had already rejected them. If I had realized back then that I should translate them into English and submit to international markets instead, I could have saved myself from a lot of that self-doubt.

You can get anyone to blurb your next book, who is it and what do they say?

Stephen King is the obvious choice, because don't we all dream about a blurb from him? I could also mention the brilliant Laura Purcell and equally brilliant Camilla Bruce. I have no idea what they would say, though... Something nice, preferably.

Do you see yourself settling into being a novelist first in the future, or do you think short stories will always play a major role in your writing?

I think I'll always return to writing short stories, though I may not write as many a year as I have up until now. Short stories are so much fun, and I think it's important to take a break from a huge project now and then and write something entirely different.

You turn eighty and look back on your writing career, what would you like to have achieved?

I have so many ideas in my head, and I'd like to be able to look back and see that I turned at least most of them into books. Though by that time, I expect my finished story ideas have been replaced by new ones...

Who/what are some short story writers/collections that you think everyone should check out?

Some collections I've very much enjoyed are Cursed Bunny by Bora Chung, Things We Say in the Dark by Kirsty Logan, What Is Not Yours Is Not Yours by Helen Oyeyemi, and above all I have to mention Wormwood by Poppy Z. Brite, who was my favorite horror author when I was a teenager.

What are you working on right now?

I'm editing a horror novel in Swedish about a young man who hires a medium to help investigate his sister's death.

Thank you, Elin! Now off with you.

More To Read

FURTHER EDITIONS OF TFBPRESENTS

Ai Jiang's Smol Tales From Between Worlds

Samantha Kolesnik's Lonesome Haunts

ALSO BY ELIN OLAUSSON

Growth

OTHER TFB RELEASES

Tales From Between: A Strange Literary Journal 1

Tales From Between: Words & Pictures

Join Us

PATREON Join our Patreon and support this publication. It also acts as an eBook subscription to everything we publish.

Support new writing: patreon.com/TalesFromBetween

TWITTER @from_between

INSTAGRAM @tales_from_between

CONTACT frombetween@gmail.com

www.ingramcontent.com/pod-product-compliance
Ingram Content Group UK Ltd.
Pitfield, Milton Keynes, MK11 3LW, UK
UKHW040009200726
13854UKWH00001B/116

9 798223 701903